Book/Accompaniment Audio

SOLOS
for the
HORN PLAYER

With Piano Accompaniment

Selected and Edited by

MASON JONES

On the accompaniment recording:

JEANNIE YU and VINCENT FUH

To access companion recorded piano accompaniments online, visit:
www.halleonard.com/mylibrary

Enter Code
3190-0596-9935-6312

If you require a physical CD of the online audio that accompanies this book, please contact Hal Leonard Corporation at info@halleonard.com.
ED 2462-B

ISBN 978-1-61780-623-0

G. SCHIRMER, Inc.

DISTRIBUTED BY

7777 W. BLUEMOUND RD. P.O. BOX 13819 MILWAUKEE, WI 53213

Copyright © 2011 by G. Schirmer, Inc. (ASCAP), New York, NY
International Copyright Secured. All Rights Reserved.
Warning: Unauthorized reproduction of this publication is
prohibited by Federal law and subject to criminal prosecution.

www.schirmer.com
www.halleonard.com

NOTE

This collection of French horn music offers a variety of solos for the horn player. Its material ranges from the seventeenth century *Kirchen Arie* of Stradella to the contemporary Largo and Allegro by Frackenpohl.

A great deal of French horn music is written to bring out the romantic and lyric nature of the instrument. While music of this type is included here, I have added some Scherzi of Beethoven and Brahms, who utilized so effectively the fanfare-like aspects of the horn.

Old friends such as Glazunov and Dukas are present as well as some new ones—Lefebvre and Labor.

Each composer selected has an original, personal gift in writing for the instrument, but whether the music is slow and contemplative or brash and shouting, the poetry of the horn is always evident. This gamut of expression is latent in this collection and is ready to be recreated by the player.

I wish to thank Mr. Vlamir Sokoloff for his valuable assistance in preparing some of the piano parts.

MASON JONES

CONTENTS

Page

1	Aria (Kirchen Arie) [1]	Alessandro Stradella
5	I Attempt from Love's Sickness to Fly [2]	Henry Purcell
9	I See a Huntsman from *Julius Caesar* [2]	George Frideric Handel
14	Rondo from Horn Quintet, K407 [2]	Wolfgang Amadeus Mozart
23	Scherzo from Septet, Op. 20 [1]	Ludwig van Beethoven
28	Andante from Symphony No. 5, "Reformation" [1]	Felix Mendelssohn
31	Scherzo from Serenade in D, Op. 11 [2]	Johannes Brahms
35	Romance, Op. 36 [2]	Camille Saint-Saëns
39	Theme and Variations, Op. 10 [1]	Josef Labor
53	Romance, Op. 30 [1]	Charles Lefebvre
61	Reveries, Op. 24 [1]	Alexander Glazunov
65	Villanelle [2]	Paul Dukas
81	Pavane pour une Infante défunte [1]	Maurice Ravel
	Largo and Allegro [1]	Arthur Frackenpohl
87	I. Largo	
91	II. Allegro	

Pianists on the recording:
[1] Jeannie Yu
[2] Vincent Fuh

The price of this publication includes access to companion recorded accompaniments online, for download or streaming, using the unique code found on the title page.

Visit www.halleonard.com/mylibrary and enter the access code.

1. Aria
(Kirchen Arie)

Arranged by Mason Jones

Alessandro Stradella
(1639–1682)

2. I Attempt from Love's Sickness to Fly

Arranged by Mason Jones

Henry Purcell
(1659–1695)

3. I See a Huntsman
from *Julius Caesar*

Arranged by Mason Jones

George Frideric Handel
(1685–1759)

4. Rondo
from Horn Quintet, K407

Arranged by Mason Jones

Wolfgang Amadeus Mozart
(1756–1791)

5. Scherzo
from Septet, Op. 20

Arranged by Mason Jones

Ludwig van Beethoven
(1770–1827)

24

26

6. Andante
from Symphony No. 5, "Reformation"

Arranged by Mason Jones

Felix Mendelssohn
(1809–1847)

7. Scherzo
from Serenade in D, Op. 11

Arranged by Mason Jones

Johannes Brahms
(1833–1897)

8. Romance
Op. 36

Camille Saint-Saëns
(1835–1921)

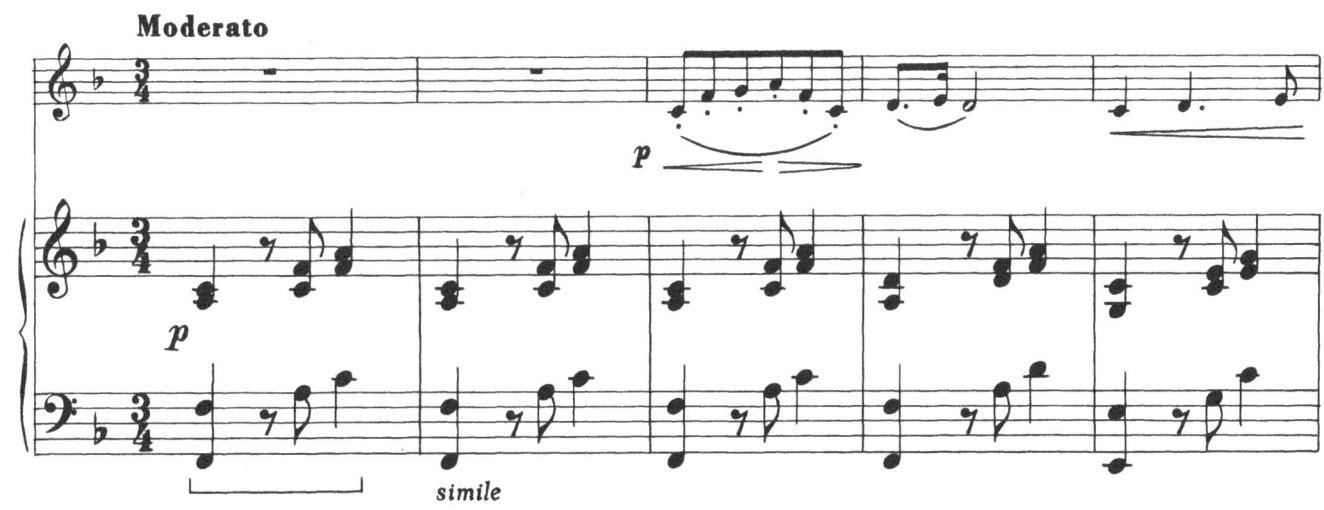

9. Theme and Variations
Op. 10

Josef Labor
(1842–1924)

44

Book/Accompaniment Audio

Horn Part

SOLOS
for the
HORN PLAYER

With Piano Accompaniment

Selected and Edited by

MASON JONES

On the accompaniment recording:

JEANNIE YU and VINCENT FUH

ED 2462-B

ISBN 978-1-61780-623-0

G. SCHIRMER, Inc.

DISTRIBUTED BY

7777 W. BLUEMOUND RD. P.O. BOX 13819 MILWAUKEE, WI 53213

Copyright © 2011 by G. Schirmer, Inc. (ASCAP), New York, NY
International Copyright Secured. All Rights Reserved.
Warning: Unauthorized reproduction of this publication is
prohibited by Federal law and subject to criminal prosecution.

www.schirmer.com
www.halleonard.com

NOTE

This collection of French horn music offers a variety of solos for the horn player. Its material ranges from the seventeenth century *Kirchen Arie* of Stradella to the contemporary Largo and Allegro by Frackenpohl.

A great deal of French horn music is written to bring out the romantic and lyric nature of the instrument. While music of this type is included here, I have added some Scherzi of Beethoven and Brahms, who utilized so effectively the fanfare-like aspects of the horn.

Old friends such as Glazunov and Dukas are present as well as some new ones—Lefebvre and Labor.

Each composer selected has an original, personal gift in writing for the instrument, but whether the music is slow and contemplative or brash and shouting, the poetry of the horn is always evident. This gamut of expression is latent in this collection and is ready to be recreated by the player.

I wish to thank Mr. Vlamir Sokoloff for his valuable assistance in preparing some of the piano parts.

MASON JONES

CONTENTS

Page

4	Aria (Kirchen Arie) [1]	Alessandro Stradella
5	I Attempt from Love's Sickness to Fly [2]	Henry Purcell
6	I See a Huntsman from *Julius Caesar* [2]	George Frideric Handel
7	Rondo from Horn Quintet, K407 [2]	Wolfgang Amadeus Mozart
10	Scherzo from Septet, Op. 20 [1]	Ludwig van Beethoven
12	Andante from Symphony No. 5, "Reformation" [1]	Felix Mendelssohn
13	Scherzo from Serenade in D, Op. 11 [2]	Johannes Brahms
14	Romance, Op. 36 [2]	Camille Saint-Saëns
16	Theme and Variations, Op. 10 [1]	Josef Labor
20	Romance, Op. 30 [1]	Charles Lefebvre
22	Reveries, Op. 24 [1]	Alexander Glazunov
23	Villanelle [2]	Paul Dukas
28	Pavane pour une Infante défunte [1]	Maurice Ravel
	Largo and Allegro [1]	Arthur Frackenpohl
29	I. Largo	
30	II. Allegro	

Pianists on the recording:
[1] Jeannie Yu
[2] Vincent Fuh

The price of this publication includes access to companion recorded accompaniments online, for download or streaming, using the unique code found on the title page.

Visit www.halleonard.com/mylibrary and enter the access code.

1. Aria
(Kirchen Arie)

Arranged by Mason Jones

Alessandro Stradella
(1639–1682)

Copyright © 1962 by G. Schirmer, Inc. (ASCAP) New York, NY
International Copyright Secured. All Rights Reserved.

2. I Attempt from Love's Sickness to Fly

Arranged by Mason Jones

Henry Purcell
(1659–1695)

3. I See a Huntsman
from *Julius Caesar*

Arranged by Mason Jones

George Frideric Handel
(1685–1759)

4. Rondo
from Horn Quintet, K407

Arranged by Mason Jones

Wolfgang Amadeus Mozart
(1756–1791)

The pianist plays the following as an introduction on the accompaniment track:

5. Scherzo
from Septet, Op. 20

Arranged by Mason Jones

Ludwig van Beethoven
(1770–1827)

The pianist plays measures 15-16 as an introduction on the accompaniment track.

6. Andante
from Symphony No. 5, "Reformation"

Arranged by Mason Jones

Felix Mendelssohn
(1809–1847)

7. Scherzo
from Serenade in D, Op. 11

Arranged by Mason Jones

Johannes Brahms
(1833–1897)

The pianist plays measures 15-16 as an introduction on the accompaniment track.

8. Romance
Op. 36

Camille Saint-Saëns
(1835–1921)

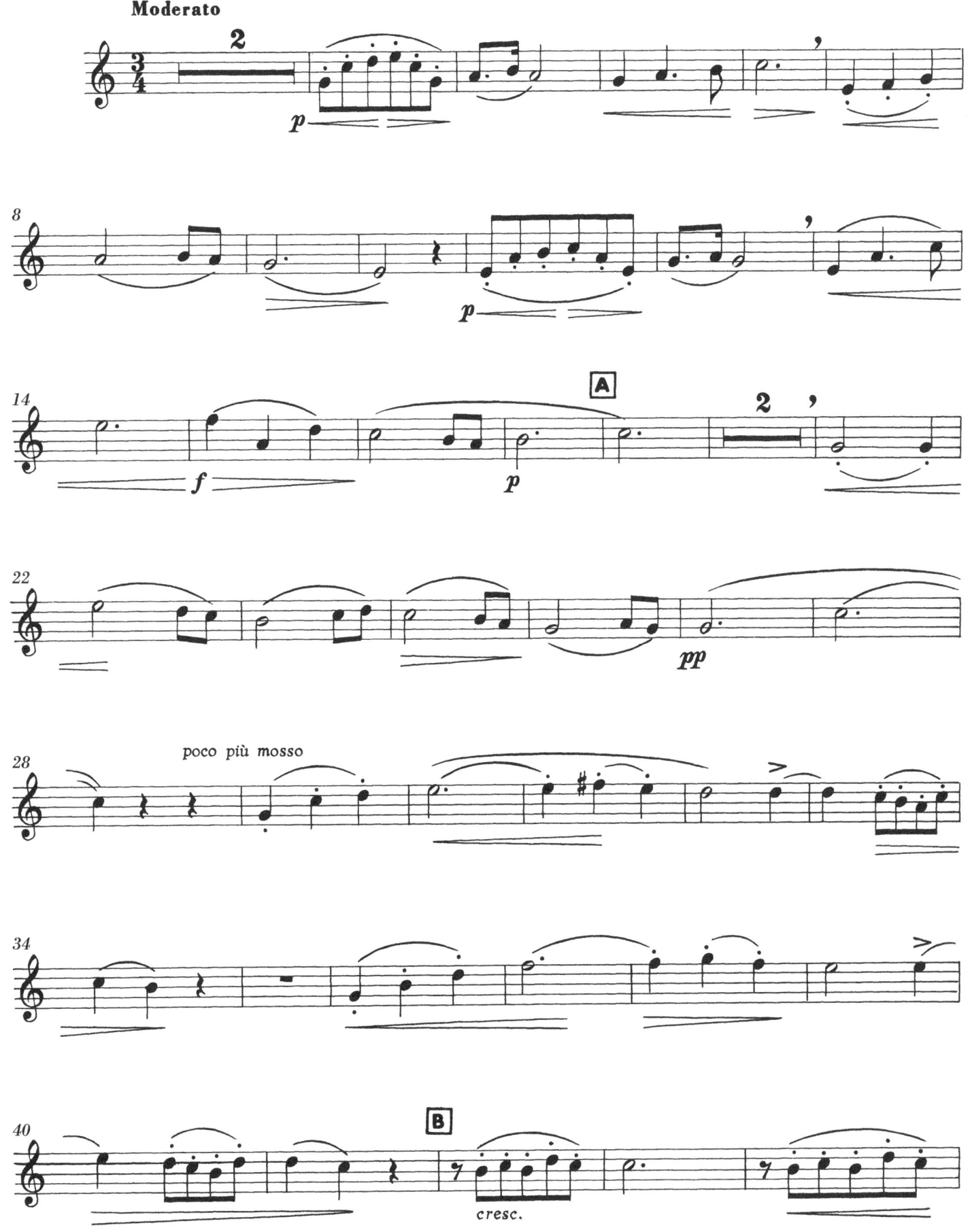

9. Theme and Variations
Op. 10

Josef Labor
(1842–1924)

10. Romance
Op. 30

Charles Lefebvre
(1843–1917)

11. Reveries
Op. 24

Alexander Glazunov
(1865–1936)

12. Villanelle

Paul Dukas
(1865–1935)

13. Pavane pour une Infante défunte

Arranged by Mason Jones

Maurice Ravel
(1875–1937)

The pianist plays measure 1 as an introduction on the accompaniment track.

14. Largo and Allegro
I. Largo

Arthur Frackenpohl
(b. 1924)

Copyright © 1962 by G. Schirmer, Inc. (ASCAP) New York, NY
International Copyright Secured. All Rights Reserved.

46

10. Romance
Op. 30

Charles Lefebvre
(1843–1917)

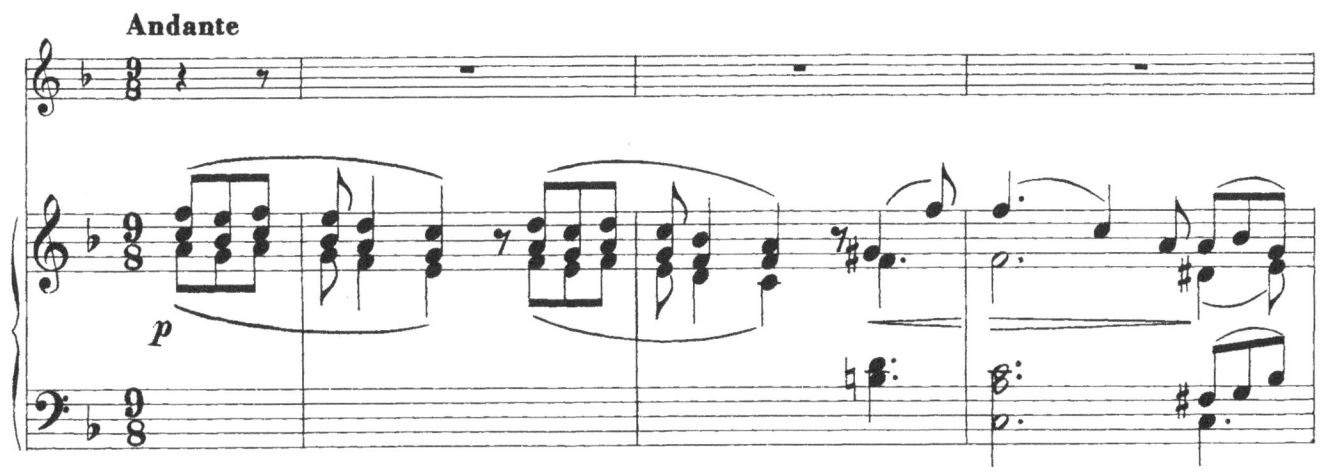

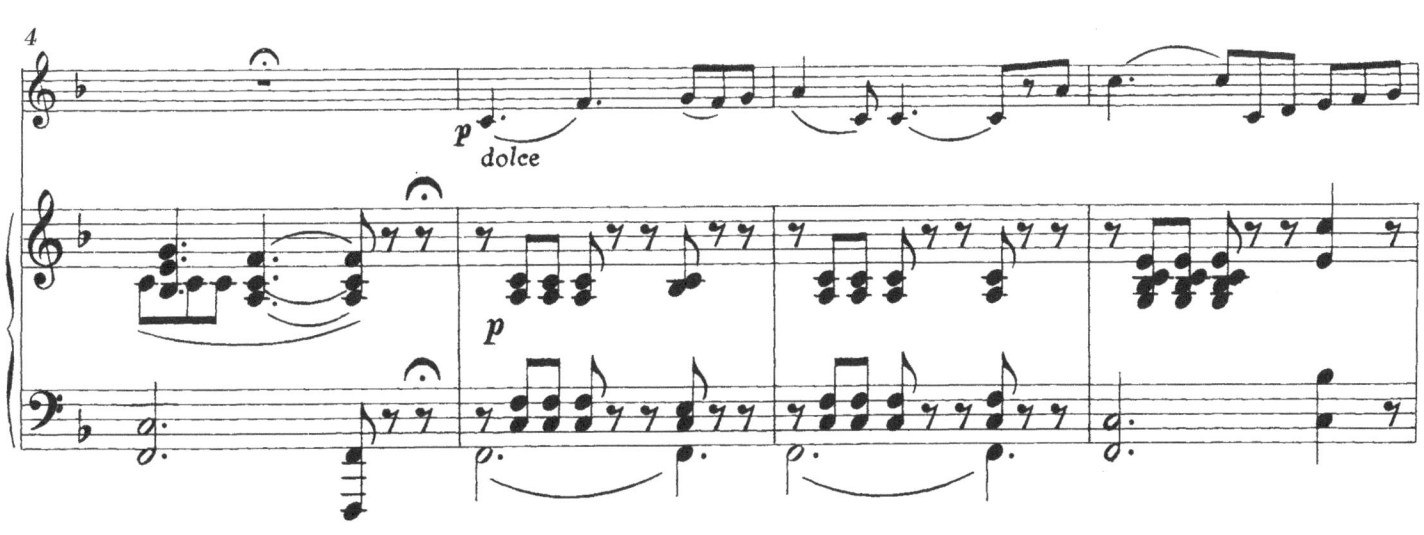

54

56

11. Reveries
Op. 24

Alexander Glazunov
(1865–1936)

64

12. Villanelle

Paul Dukas
(1865–1935)

66

68

74

13. Pavane pour une Infante défunte

Arranged by Mason Jones

Maurice Ravel
(1875–1937)

14. Largo and Allegro

I. Largo

Arthur Frackenpohl
(b. 1924)

A version of this work for horn and string orchestra is available on rental from G. Schirmer, Inc.

Copyright © 1962 by G. Schirmer, Inc. (ASCAP) New York, NY
International Copyright Secured. All Rights Reserved.

88

II. Allegro

94